© 1995 Geddes & Grosset Ltd
Published by Geddes & Grosset Ltd,
New Lanark, Scotland.

ISBN 1 85534 594 3

Printed and bound in China.

10 9 8 7 6 5 4 3 2

The Princess and the Pea

Retold by Judy Hamilton
Illustrated by Lindsay Duff

Tarantula Books

L ong ago, in a far distant kingdom, there lived a king and queen and their young son, the prince. The king and queen were very proud of their son. He was their only child, and as far as his parents were concerned, nothing was too good for him. From the day that he was born, the boy was given the very best of everything; he wore the finest clothes, he ate the choicest of foods, he had the noblest of horses to ride and he had the best of teachers. The prince grew up tall and strong, a credit to his parents. He was clever and good-natured and handsome.

When the prince had grown up, he began to think that it was about time that he found a girl to love and to marry. Of course, such a fine young man was very popular, and there were many young ladies from noble families in the kingdom who would have dearly loved to become the prince's wife. In other kingdoms near and far as well, word had spread of the prince, and there too were many young ladies who would give anything to become his bride. But the queen, still determined that only the very best was good enough for her son, told him:

"When you marry, my son, you must marry a true princess. No-one else will be good enough."

The prince came from a very old and respected royal family and could understand why his mother wanted him to marry a true princess, so he told her that he would only consider courting young ladies who came from other royal families. But this did not satisfy the queen.

"These young ladies may come from royal families," she said, "but they may still not be TRUE princesses. You must marry a TRUE princess."

"How shall I be able to tell who is and who is not a TRUE princess?" the prince wanted to know.

"Trust me, my son. I shall find you a true princess to marry," said his mother.

In the days that followed, the queen sent out messengers near and far to make it known that the prince was looking for a princess to marry. Any young ladies of royal blood who wanted to be considered as a possible bride for the prince were to make their wishes known to the palace. Every one would be invited to the palace in turn to spend one night in the guest suite. The royal family would then be able to make a decision about who would be honoured by becoming the prince's bride.

The announcement also stated that only true princesses would be considered.

The messengers all set off on their journeys, and the queen gathered her servants together to prepare the guest suite in the palace. The rooms were very grand already, and the bedroom had in it a large and comfortable bed with a soft feather mattress, but the queen did not appear to think that it was comfortable enough. She ordered her puzzled servants to bring in nineteen more mattresses and to pile them, one on top of another, onto the guest bed. With twenty mattresses on it, the bed was so high that a ladder was needed to get into it! But the queen was satisfied. When no-one was looking, she slipped a single pea underneath the mattress that lay at the very bottom of the pile.

Life was very busy in the palace during the coming weeks. Countless young ladies wanted to marry the prince. Every night, another carriage would drive through the palace gates with another hopeful bride-to-be. Each guest was treated with the greatest of kindness and courtesy. All of them were given the same chance to convince the queen that they would make a suitable bride for her son. As they all claimed to be of royal birth they were all asked the most careful questions about their families to make sure that they were telling the truth. After being given a sumptuous dinner, each princess was then shown to the guest suite to spend the night before returning home.

Weeks passed, and many princesses came to visit the palace. Some were beautiful, some were very charming and witty. Most of them came from royal families. The prince spent time with each, and there were some whom he liked very much. But according to the queen, none of them was a TRUE princess. The morning after a guest had spent the night in the palace, she would ask each one the same question:

"Did you sleep well last night?"

And each girl would reply politely:

"Yes, thank you, your majesty, I slept well."

Then the queen would frown and when the girl left, she would turn to her son and say:

"She was not a TRUE princess."

The prince was very puzzled. How could his mother tell that all these young ladies were not TRUE princesses? Was royal blood not enough? But the queen was a strong woman. The prince dared not argue. The queen sent messengers even farther away than before in search of a TRUE princess.

As time passed, the flow of visitors to the castle began to slow down. The number of princesses coming to see the prince became smaller and smaller. It began to seem as if they would never find a TRUE princess. The prince felt very depressed. He wanted so much to find someone to marry. Now it seemed as if they had run out of places to look for a bride for him!

After some time, the flow of visitors to the castle stopped altogether. Weeks went by, and the prince felt sure he would never marry now, but the queen told him not to worry.

"Your princess will come one day, wait and see!" she said.

One dark and stormy night, the prince was listening to the wind howl outside, and feeling very gloomy, when there was a knock on the door of the palace. The prince followed the servant who went to open the door and saw a very bedraggled young woman standing in the doorway.

"I am very cold and wet," she said. "May I stay here for the night until the storm dies down?"

The prince took pity on the girl and showed her into the great hall. He ordered hot food and some wine for her. While she ate her meal by the fire, the prince sat beside her and they talked. He noticed that the girl's clothes were threadbare and her shoes worn out, and asked where she came from.

"I was brought up by a poor old woman in a village far from here," the girl said. "She found me in the forest when I was a baby. She tells me I am a princess from a distant kingdom."

The prince became quite excited. Could this girl be a TRUE princess? She was very beautiful, even in her old clothes, and very charming. He went to tell the queen.

The queen said that the girl could stay the night. The prince was delighted. The girl looked worn out, so he showed her to the guest suite and said goodnight, leaving her to climb the ladder to the top of the pile of mattresses.

The next morning at breakfast, the poor girl looked even more tired than before. The prince felt sorry for her. The queen asked her if she had slept well. The girl hesitated:

"I hate to be rude, your majesty, but I cannot lie. The bed looked comfortable, but it felt so lumpy that I could not sleep a wink!" The queen, surprisingly, looked very pleased!

"My son, at last we have found a TRUE princess!" she told the prince.

The prince was happy. He knew he loved the girl. But he was puzzled.

"How do you know that she is a TRUE princess?" he asked his mother. His mother smiled, and took the prince and the girl to the guest suite. From beneath the pile of mattresses, she took out the pea and showed it to them both.

"Only a TRUE princess could feel this under twenty feather mattresses," she said.

The prince and the TRUE princess laughed at the queen's cunning. Then the prince asked the TRUE princess to marry him. She agreed, and they went to tell the king to make preparations for a great wedding celebration. It was the start of a long and very happy life together.